The Most Beautiful Kid in the World

JENNIFER A. ERICSSON

Pictures by SUSAN MEDDAUGH

TAMBOURINE BOOKS NEW YORK

Printed in Hong Kong by South China Printing Company (1988) Ltd.
The text type is Zapf International.
The illustrations were prepared using watercolor and colored pencils.

Library of Congress Cataloging in Publication Data
Ericsson, Jennifer A.
The most beautiful kid in the world / by Jennifer A. Ericsson ;
pictures by Susan Meddaugh.—1st ed.
p. cm.
Summary: At the last minute, Annie takes off her conventional clothes in a
sudden burst of desire to dress far more unconventionally but
comfortably for her grandmother's visit.
[1. Grandmothers—Fiction. 2. Clothing and dress—Fiction.]
I. Meddaugh, Susan, ill. II. Title.
PZ7.72584Mo 1996 [Fic]—dc20 95-53063 CIP AC
ISBN 0-688-13941-8 (tr.)—ISBN 0-688-13942-6 (lib. bdg.)
3 5 7 9 10 8 6 4
First edition

To Annie, the most beautiful kid in my world
J.A.E.

For Meera
S.M.

Grandma is coming for dinner tonight. I want to be beautiful—the most beautiful kid in the world!

But I don't feel beautiful.

My shoes pinch. My tights droop.

And the tag on my dress scratches my neck.

"Mama, can't I wear something else?"

"Oh, honey, Grandma will love that dress."

"Please, Mama . . ."

Mama sighs. "I want you to look nice tonight, Annie.

It's Grandma's birthday."

"I'll be the most beautiful kid in the world!"

I race down the hall to my room.

Kick . . . off with the shoes!

Rip . . . off with the tights!

Yank . . . that dress comes over my head!

READ!

I dig in my bottom drawer.

S-t-r-e-t-c-h . . . S-t-r-e-t-c-h . . .

I'm warm and comfortable

in my flowery long underwear.

My jean jumper?

My short skirt?

I know!

I grab my ballet bag out of the closet.

Zip! Wiggle! Twirl!

"How are you doing, Annie?" calls Mama.

"Fine, Mama, just fine."

Knee socks?

Sandals?

No . . . white ruffled Sunday socks.

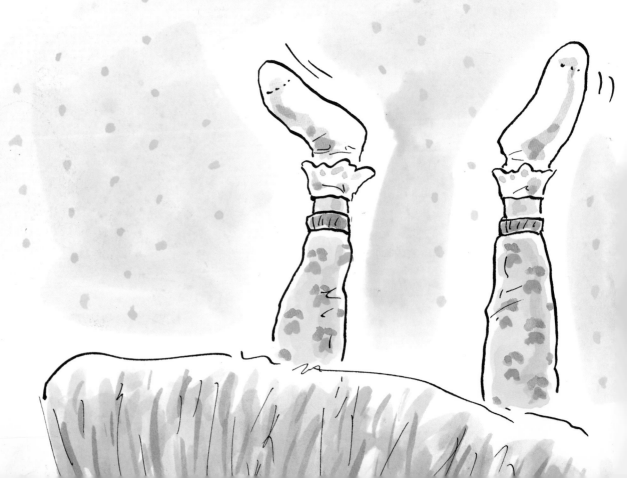

And my red Rollerblades . . .

are under here somewhere.

ROLL RUMBLE ZOOOM

"Don't you dare, Annie!" calls Mama.

Rats!

I slip them off and scoot into the bathroom.

A ponytail over here . . .

one over here . . . one way back here . . .
and one in the front. Perfect!

Mama knocks on the door. She turns the knob.

"Are you ready?"

"Not yet! Not yet!"

Brrring! Saved by the phone!

"Hurry up," warns Mama as she runs to answer it.

I tuck a silver crown into my hair. Then I peek out into the hallway. Mama is still talking, so I dash to her room.

A squirt of perfume.

Sparkling earrings.

A long string of pearls.

And Daddy's favorite slippers.

Yes!

Some lipstick—

Yuck!

I grab a tissue and wipe it away.

"Let's see how you look, Annie," calls Mama.

"Just a second!"

I tiptoe to the kitchen.

The cabinet door squeaks as I pull it open.

"Are you all set?" calls Mama.

"Almost."

I open the peanut butter jar
and spread some on my lips.

Just as I finish,

the doorbell rings.

"I'll get it!"

Scuff . . . scuff . . . scuff, scuff, scuff.

I grab the knob and fling the door open.

"Happy birthday, Grandma!"

Grandma opens her arms wide.

"Why, you're the most beautiful kid in the world!"

And I *am*—as I give her a great big peanut butter kiss.